Samantha

One Finger, One Nose,
A Whole Lot Of Bugs

Written by Dave Diggle

Illustrated by Sarah Preuss

Also by Dave Diggle:

Alfie: Learns When Poo Just Isn't Cool Anymore
Annie: A Small Ant With Some Big Questions
Barbara: A Sssslithering Adventure Of Self Discovery
Bella: Shares Her Sticky Plan
Boris: The Eight Legged Manners Maestro
Brian: Eats Himself Smarter
Cyril: Finds His Place In The Family Tree
Douglas: Pays The Price For Not Paying Attention
Ewan: From Bullied To Superhero In One Afternoon
Frederick: Thinking Makes Breathing Easy
George and Toby: Won't Have A Baaa Of Bed-Wetting
Lilly: The Crazy Little Van
Malana: Learns When Enough Is Enough
Mary: A Birds Eye View On The Dangers Of Strangers
Melanie: Honestly Finds Herself Out Of Her Depth
Paco: The High-Performance Penguin
Reggie: Learns To Roll With It
Sally: And Her Singing Stage Debut
Sammy: Leaves His Mark

First edition published 2008 by Diggle de Doo™ Australia
ISBN 9780977510474
www.digglededoo.com.au

© Diggle de Doo™ Productions Pty Ltd 2008-2011

Suitable For Ages 4-8 years

National Library of Australia Cataloguing-in-Publication entry

Author:	Diggle, Dave.
Title:	Samantha : one finger, one nose, a whole lot of bugs / written by Dave Diggle ; illustrated by Sarah Preuss.
ISBN:	9780987165800 (pbk.)
Target Audience:	For primary school age.
Subjects:	Nose--Juvenile fiction.
	Hygiene--Juvenile fiction.
Other Authors/ Contributors:	Preuss, Sarah.
Dewey Number:	A823.4

Illustrations, cover design and internal layout by Sarah Preuss

Dedicated to my beautiful
and inspiring children
Jack, Holly and Chloe

Why use metaphors?

Metaphors occur when one object is likened to another. In storytelling, metaphors can be used to create a meaningful connection between the message being delivered and one's own personal experience.

One of our greatest attributes when we are young is our unrestricted imagination. A world of endless possibilities is ours to explore.

It is with this imagination that we become our own super heroes, fighting evil and feeling confident, safe and untouchable — no matter what the reality of our circumstances are at the time.

For some of us, it is pure, unbridled imagination; for others, it is an escape from undesirable circumstances.

The difference between the adult's and child's coping mechanism is that we as adults, based on our many years of experience, apply deductive logic to situations, attempting to justify and reason with issues within the boundaries of conscious logic.

Children do not have the benefit of so many years of experience, so they tend to look for a safe alternative to control the situation in their own way. A child's spirit of adventure will always find its own happy ending no matter how far fetched it may appear.

Inspire, motivate, support, guide, cherish and nurture. These are all things we want to do for children — and never more so than when we are faced with a child with a problem.

A simple, elegant way to deal with many of these childhood issues is through the use of metaphor. A well-constructed metaphor offers a non-confronting alternate solution to an issue by passively guiding the child through a story to find their own conclusions.

Metaphors bring imagination to life. The key to the metaphors in this collection is that one story can captivate so many imaginations simultaneously. The stories are abstract to the level where children create personal connections to the stories and attribute their own meanings, and therefore take control and come to their own solutions.

◎ ◎ ◎

This book is a collection of metaphors for helping children deal with some common life issues. This book is designed for the metaphor to be read to the child to allow the bright, vibrant illustrations and the use of specific language patterns weaved throughout to draw everyone in and be part of the adventure.

People tend to search for their own answers. As they search, they attribute their own meaning to things. Children are no different.

As you read each story, in the child's mind associations are created to the story's message. Each metaphor gently guides the child through an adventure with the characters, opening up new possibilities to them and leading them to a desirable conclusion. Subconsciously, the mind processes and creates its own individual solution.

So hop in and enjoy the ride as we teach our children through their own imagination...

Samantha Piggleton of Pickwick Lane is just like your average six-year-old girl.

She loves to play with her dolls and they have tea parties in the garden every Sunday afternoon. She also plays dress-up with her mum's old clothes, dressing herself and her dolls most elegantly.

Best of all, she loves going shopping with her mum for new clothes as she likes to look pretty and cool.

Samantha also likes to wear her blonde hair in pigtails with her neatly cut fringe sitting just above the rim of her glasses. You see, she is just like any normal six-year-old girl.

Samantha did, however, have a dark secret, an unpleasant habit and one which she didn't appear to be too concerned about. One, however, that puts a shiver down the spine of anyone who would catch a glimpse of her doing it.

You see, Samantha used to like to pick her nose. Not just pick it; she would dig deep, rummage around and explore. She picked it when it was itchy, she picked it when it was blocked, she even picked it when—well, whenever she wanted to really.

Of course, her mum and dad would always say it wasn't very nice or ladylike to pick your nose, as you never know where your grubby fingers have been.

Samantha never used to take any notice of her mum and dad. She would tut, raise her eyebrows and just look at them with a finger up her nose in defiance.

Yuck!

One day as Samantha was serving tea at her doll's party, she was explaining to them, "The price of tea was awful these days due to the price of..."

Samantha stopped in mid-sentence.

She got a tingle. Then the tingle became a twitch, the twitch became a buzzing and the buzzing became an uncontrollable urge to pick—THUMP! Her finger went up her nose.

"Ahhh," she sighed as she slumped back into her pink beanbag with her eyes closed and her finger wedged deep into her left nostril.

When Samantha finished the rummage of her nose, she attempted to remove her finger for a closer examination, only to find it was stuck!

The harder she pulled, the more stuck it became. Samantha twisted it, wiggled it and pulled it. Nothing budged. She even pushed deeper to see if she could free the lodged finger from her nose.

Still nothing moved.

So, Samantha Piggleton of Pickwick Lane's finger was stuck up her nose... and stuck good.

"What am I to do?" she mumbled. She began to panic as she looked in the mirror.

What she did not realise were bugs from the planet Grubdem had snuck onto Samantha's fingers whilst she was serving tea at her garden tea party.

They snuck onto her fingers and had hidden under her fingernails.

And so when Samantha picked her nose, the bugs seized their opportunity to come out of hiding—like pirates on a ghost ship—and quickly anchored her finger right at the top of her nostril, cheering heartily as they did. They did this by tying off tiny ropes with anchors, just as real pirates would.

They set up base camp on the warm slippery surface at the back of Samantha's nose, whilst splitting into teams to explore the inside of Samantha's head.

Bugs being bugs, they multiplied very quickly into three teams. Team Three were to explore the depths of Samantha's throat. Team Two were off to explore Samantha's ears and Team One had the difficult and dangerous job of exploring Samantha's brain.

And so off they went. Team Three, lead by the famed explorer Sir Winston Bug, tied ropes to the hairs on the inside of Samantha's nose. Sir Winston was then lowered all the way down to the back of her throat on a wooden plank before landing on the back of her soft tongue with a dull thud.

When they arrived, they set up another camp and had a picnic, as bugs love to eat... and they do eat lots.

Sir Winston Bug then set about collecting samples from Samantha's throat to use in his research laboratory back on the planet Grubdem. He scraped samples from the walls of Samantha's throat, her tonsils (the ball like things) and the long dangly thing right at the back of her throat, which nobody seems to know the name of, leaving them all looking rather red and sore.

Sir Winston Bug then collected all his sample jars, packing them away very carefully before starting back up Samantha's throat and back to base camp.

They stomped their dirty big boots all over the place as they left, leaving their rubbish from their picnic too.

By this time Team Two, led by Madam Hillary Bug, had arrived in Samantha's right ear. Again, they set up camp and proceeded to enjoy a very large picnic. The Grubdem Bug picnics are not like the sort of picnic you and I might enjoy. These bugs feast on slime, grime and gunk, and lots of it.

This is the staple diet of all bugs from the planet Grubdem, and to be honest with you, their manners left a lot to be desired, throwing away whatever didn't go into their mouths.

Madam Hillary Bug began conducting sound tests on Samantha's eardrum. She began by hitting the inside of Samantha's ear as hard as she could with a big bug hammer. Then she hit it as fast as she could, before finally running all eight of her nails at the end of her long legs down the eardrum, making an awful screeching sound like fingernails on a blackboard.

This left Samantha's ears looking very red and feeling very sore.

Happy with her experiments, Madam Hillary collected the test results and made her way back to base camp to join Sir Winston Bug, who was again enjoying his second picnic for the day.

Of course, whilst all this was going on, Team One, led by the expedition leader Colonel Barnaby Bug, were making their way through Samantha's head, stomping all through the sqwidgy outer layer of her brain in their dirty gumboots. They were collecting samples along the way and leaving their rubbish too. A fair exchange thought Colonel Barnaby bug. It was like a dirty river when they had finished, with rubbish floating all around them. One bug had even lost his gumboot in all the sludge.

Samantha had rushed down to tell her mum and dad that she could not get her finger out of her nose. Samantha had a very worried look on her face and tears welling in her eyes as she ran into the kitchen where her mum and dad were enjoying a cup of tea.

"Mum, Dad, it's stuck," she muffled, as it is very hard to be heard clearly with a finger up your nose.

"Oh dear," said Mrs Piggleton, putting down her cup of tea. "What are we to do?"

First, Mrs Piggleton tried pulling Samantha's finger as hard as she could. With one foot on the kitchen sink and her hands gripped tightly on Samantha's arm, she pulled and pulled. This only brought more tears to Samantha's eyes, as the pulling was pulling on the anchors in her nose.

"Ouch, ouch, ooooouch," said Samantha.

"This just isn't working," sighed Mrs Piggleton.

Mr Piggleton got out his big red toolbox, removed a large torch, a set of long nose pliers and a hammer before going to the refrigerator and removing some butter, just like a doctor would—well, almost!

"You hold her down," he said to Mrs Piggleton with a stern look on his face, "and I will pull, twist and lever."

Samantha screamed, "Noooooooooooooo!" before running up the stairs to her bedroom and locking the door behind her.

Samantha began to cry. She thought that perhaps she would have to spend the rest of her life with a finger stuck up her nose. She then thought how the other children at school might laugh at her.

Suddenly, Samantha got a tingle... Then the tingle became a twitch, the twitch became a buzzing and the buzzing became a huge sneeze, blowing the finger right out of Samantha's nose along with the planet Grubdem bugs who had hidden under Samantha's fingernails once again with their collected samples and full tummies.

Samantha was ecstatic. She ran downstairs to show her mum and dad that she had removed her stuck finger. "Without butter, pliers or a hammer, thank you very much," she finished.

Mr and Mrs Piggleton looked up. As they were busy hatching another plan to help Samantha by collecting items, such as the sink plunger, bars of soap and the pepper grinder.

Very relieved, Mrs Piggleton hugged Samantha, as secretly she didn't think the plunger, soap and pepper grinder would have worked.

Mr Piggleton began putting the items back into his tool box, "I am sure the pepper would have been the clincher," he said.

That night as Samantha lay in her bed she began to feel a little unwell. 'Maybe I am getting a cold,' she thought to herself.

Her nose was very red with lots and lots of goop running out of it and very sore. Her throat was scratchy, her ears ached and her head was hot and throbbing.

Maybe, just maybe, the litter from those Grubdem bugs and their picnics had made Samantha sick.

Who knows? Although it is probably best not to let them in there again next time.

Samantha decided she wasn't going to pick her nose again, as she didn't really know where her grubby fingers had been.

Do you?

Thank you to my loving wife and business partner, Linda.

I could not have achieved this without your love,
understanding and swift kicks along the way.

25827070R00016

Printed in Poland
by Amazon Fulfillment
Poland Sp. z o.o., Wrocław